DO YOU ENJOY BEING ~~SCARED~~

WOULD YOU RA~~THER~~ HAVE
NIGHTM~~ARES~~
INSTEAD OF SWEET DREAMS?

ARE YOU HAPPY ONLY WHEN
SHAKING WITH FEAR?

CONGRATULATIONS ! ! ! !

YOU'VE MADE A WISE CHOICE.

THIS BOOK IS THE DOORWAY
TO ALL THAT MAY FRIGHTEN YOU.

GET READY FOR

COLD, CLAMMY SHIVERS
RUNNING UP AND DOWN YOUR SPINE!

NOW, OPEN THE DOOR–
IF YOU DARE !!!!

Shivers

THE MYSTIC'S SPELL

M. D. Spenser

Plantation, Florida

To Lisa Keller

Published by Paradise Press, Inc. by arrangement with River Publishing, Inc. All right, title and interest to the "SHIVERS" logo and design are owned by River Publishing, Inc. No portion of the "SHIVERS" logo and design may be reproduced in part or whole without prior written permission from River Publishing, Inc. An application for a registered trademark of the "SHIVERS" logo and design is pending with the Federal Patent and Trademark office.

ISBN 1-57657-052-5

EXCLUSIVE DISTRIBUTION BY PARADISE PRESS, INC.

Cover Design by George Paturzo
Cover Illustration by Eddie Roseboom

Printed in the U.S.A.

30631

THE MYSTIC'S SPELL

<u>Chapter One</u>

"Hey, Timmy, are you going to the carnival? It just came to town and it's going to be here a few days."

Timmy's best friend — in fact, his only friend — Howard, was breathing hard from running to catch up to him. School had just let out, but Timmy didn't wait for Howard to walk home with him. He wanted to get home fast, before Hank Wilson and his pals picked on him, as was their habit most days.

"Yes, I'll probably go," Timmy said.

The truth was, he wasn't so sure.

He had gone to the carnival last year when it came to town, and he hadn't much liked it. He had gone into the Haunted House with several other kids from school. He had been so frightened, he screamed and ran from the house. The others all laughed at him.

Then when Timmy went on the Tilt-A-Whirl, the spinning motion of the ride made him sick. Every-

1

body at school heard about how he threw up on himself. Hank Wilson called him "The Human Volcano," saying Timmy spewed chicken casserole instead of lava.

Now a year had passed. Timmy thought a moment. At age eleven, he told himself, he was braver and stronger than he had been a year earlier.

"Yes," he told Howard. "I'll be going to the carnival." This time he meant it.

Timmy knew that Howard was the one classmate who would not hold last year's carnival disaster against him. The two lived a block from each other and had been friends since first grade.

It wasn't easy for Timmy to make friends. He was short and thin, and often sick with colds and the flu. He had so little athletic ability that he was always the last boy chosen when teams were picked to play softball, basketball or soccer.

Even Harold, the fattest, slowest boy in class got picked for teams ahead of Timmy.

Timmy usually struck out when it was his turn to bat. When he did manage to hit the ball, it was usually a weak grounder back to the pitcher, or to the second baseman.

Last year Timmy's teacher had the boys and

girls play together on softball teams. Timmy was the only boy in his class who was not chosen for a team ahead of the girls. Even now, a year later, he was still embarrassed about it.

Timmy was, however, one of the smartest students in his class. He solved math problems quickly, but reading was his favorite subject. Why, just last month, his teacher had stood in front of the entire class and praised his book report on *To Kill A Mockingbird* as one of the finest she had ever read.

This made Timmy more unpopular than ever with boys like Hank Wilson.

Hank had curly blond hair, a sturdy build and a constant scowl on his face. He was one of the best athletes at school, and one of the meanest.

But Hank struggled with schoolwork with the same futility that Timmy showed in trying to hit a softball. It seemed to Timmy that the better he did in school, the more Hank picked on him.

Howard wasn't that way, though. He was neither a gifted athlete nor an especially bright student, but he did all right in both. An outgoing boy with a ready smile, he moved easily from one group of students to another. He was liked by everybody.

"Let's stop at the arcade on the way home,"

Howard suggested. "I'll bet I can beat you at Mortal Kombat."

Timmy and Howard often stopped at the arcade on their way home from school. Even though he was awful at sports, Timmy wasn't a bad video game and pinball player. When he played Howard, he won almost as often as he lost.

"Okay," he said. "You're on."

The arcade was in a shopping mall a few blocks from school. It was a popular hangout for kids of all ages. Timmy's mother had warned him not to spend all of his allowance there, but sometimes he did.

"You'll never guess what I heard today," Howard teased.

"What?"

"I heard that Sally kind of likes you."

"Really?"

"Really."

Timmy kind of liked Sally, too. She had red hair, pale skin and freckles. She was a good student, too. She was so quiet and shy, though, that he hardly knew her.

Timmy was thinking about this as he and Howard rounded a corner to walk down the street to the mall.

Suddenly they came face to face with Hank Wilson and his friends, Duane and Jason. All three boys had smirks on their faces.

Timmy gulped. He knew that look.

Something bad was about to happen.

<u>Chapter Two</u>

"Where do you think you're going?" Hank snarled, glaring at Timmy.

Hank stood with his hands on his hips and his chin out. His body language practically dared Timmy to keep walking.

"We're going to the arcade," Timmy replied. He tried not to sound scared, but his voice betrayed him. It sounded high and tense.

"That's funny. Me and the boys were going to go there too," Hank growled, glancing at Duane and Jason. "Only problem is, we don't have enough money. Maybe you could help us out."

Timmy knew this wasn't a suggestion. It was a demand. He had been through this before with Hank and his pals.

Several times, they had ordered him to give them his lunch money or get beaten up. He always gave them the money.

6

This time, Timmy decided not to. Maybe he felt bolder with Howard beside him. Or maybe he was just tired of giving in.

"Sorry, Hank, I can't give you any money," he said in a quavering voice. "I've only got enough for myself."

"Well then, we'll just have to help ourselves," Hank replied.

He stepped toward Timmy.

Timmy tried to run past him, but Duane and Jason grabbed him.

"Not so fast, little man," Hank laughed harshly.

"Leave him alone!" Howard shouted. His voice sounded as shrill and nervous as Timmy's.

"You stay out of this," Hank demanded.

Howard wanted to help Timmy, but he knew it was hopeless. It was three against two. And the other boys were stronger and tougher.

Howard watched helplessly.

Timmy wriggled furiously, like a fish on a hook. But he couldn't escape the clutches of Duane and Jason. One boy had him in a headlock. The other hung on to his ankles to keep him from kicking.

Hank began rifling through Timmy's pockets.

First he tried one of the back pockets on Timmy's blue cotton trousers. All that got him was a comb. Next, he tried the left front pocket. All he found there was a pencil and an eraser.

Now Hank's grasping fingers dug into the right front pocket of Timmy's pants.

"Bingo!" he yelped.

With an evil grin, Hank removed his hand from Timmy's pocket. Clutched inside it were five rumpled one dollar bills and three quarters.

"Stop it! Let me go!" cried Timmy.

"Sure, squirt," Hank cackled. "Let him go, guys."

Timmy was still struggling to get free. When Duane and Jason suddenly relaxed their grips on him, his struggling caused him to fall forward and then flat on his face.

All three of his tormentors hooted. His friend, Howard, looked embarrassed. Timmy was humiliated.

"Thanks for the donation, timid Timmy," roared Hank. "Yeah, that's what I'll call you, Timid Timmy! See you at the arcade, sport!"

As Hank and his friends skipped off down the street to the mall, Howard helped Timmy to his feet.

Timmy's face was red, his hair was mussed up

and his shirt was ripped.

"I'd give anything to be stronger than those guys!" he moaned, as tears welled up in his eyes. "Anything!"

Chapter Three

The next day at school Timmy managed to be near other kids whenever his path crossed Hank's. So Hank pretended not to see him.

Excitement of another kind, however, kept the students restless in their seats.

It was Friday. As usual, Timmy and his classmates eagerly awaited the weekend.

But this Friday held more anticipation than most. A lot of kids were planning to go to the carnival that night.

The classroom was buzzing as Timmy's classmates discussed which rides were most fun last year, and which were duds.

"I hear they've got a couple of new rides that are faster and scarier than anything there last year," announced Hank. "I'm going on those! Hey, Timmy, they've even got some kiddie rides for you!"

Timmy ignored the taunt. Instead, he asked Sally with the red hair if she was going.

Sally's face turned bright red and she looked down, pretending to find something interesting in her book.

"I might go," she said, still not looking at Timmy. Then her face flushed again.

Timmy and Howard agreed later that day that they would go, too, if they got permission from their parents.

After school, Timmy went straight home. He did not see Hank.

As Timmy walked through the front door of his house, he could hear his mother in the kitchen.

She was a small woman who wore glasses and had a curly mop of brown hair.

"Hi, Timmy! How was your day?" she asked.

"Okay," Timmy said. Then he got right to the point.

"Mom, can I go to the carnival with Howard tonight? I'll be home early."

Timmy wore what he imagined was his most sincere expression. He knew his mother was reluctant to let him go out at night without an adult. But she would be pleased he was going with Howard, whom she thought acted older than his years.

Timmy stood waiting, like a puppy hoping for a bone.

His mom thought about it a moment, then set the ground rules.

"You can go, but don't be spending all your money there," she said. "I want you home by ten o'clock. And try not to rip your clothes like you did yesterday."

After dinner, Timmy called Howard, who said he had also gotten permission to go to the carnival. Timmy changed into jeans, a long-sleeved T-shirt, a sweater and sneakers. He brushed his teeth and combed his hair.

Then he took a deep breath. He was determined to have a better time at the carnival than he had last year.

Chapter Four

The carnival was always crowded on Friday nights, and this year was no different. In some parts of the midway people were crammed shoulder to shoulder.

Teenaged boys and girls held hands, laughed and ate cotton candy and corn dogs. Parents carried small children or pushed them in strollers. Bigger children begged their parents to give them tickets for rides.

Timmy and Howard stayed to the outside of the sea of people so they could see the carnival's attractions better.

As they inched along, shouldering their way through the crowd, barkers beckoned to them from their booths.

"Over here. Come on, young man, you can win a teddy bear! All it costs is a quarter," yelled a skinny man with beady eyes who looked like a weasel. He worked at a game where a player could win a big stuffed bear by tossing a softball inside a milk canister.

Timmy looked over at the booth. He knew, from having overheard some carnival workers (or "carnies," as they called themselves) that people who worked the midway called their booths "joints."

From the rafters of the joint where the weasel-eyed man worked, giant teddies hung merrily. Some were brown, while others were purple or red. All wore green T-shirts and matching baseball caps. It seemed to Timmy as if the bears were as big as him.

Timmy wanted badly to win one of the bears. He thought of how pleased his mother would be if he gave it to her.

Or maybe he would give it to Sally. He wondered if she would turn red if he did.

Each softball cost only a quarter, but Timmy and Howard decided not to play. They knew the softball was almost as big as the mouth of the canister, making it really hard to get a ball to drop inside.

"What's the matter, you boys chicken?" the weasel-eyed carny yelled after them as they walked away.

Timmy and Howard were swept up again in

the swarm of people walking the midway. Off to the left, the horses on a carousel spun by, a blur of color and music.

To the right, barkers from other games shouted and begged.

"Come on boys, give it a try! Step right up!"

From somewhere else, Timmy could hear a barker at the haunted house hissing into a microphone.

"Venture inside if you dare," he growled. "Especially if you want a scare."

People towered over Timmy on every side. He looked up to see a man carrying his little boy on his shoulders. As he turned his head to watch, a woman's purse bopped him in the face.

The noise. The colors. The people. Everything swirled around Timmy. He felt dizzy.

"I need to sit down a minute," he said woozily.

He and Howard walked a few yards off the midway, to a spot where it was not so crowded. After a couple of minutes, Timmy felt better.

Nearby stood a big bearded man wearing faded jeans, a tuxedo shirt and a top hat. Behind him were some shelves with small toys. On top of the shelves was a battered white sign with big red letters that read: "Fool The Guesser."

For one dollar, The Guesser said he could guess a person's age within one year, or weight within five pounds.

Timmy decided to try and fool The Guesser. He figured it would be harder to figure out his weight than his age, so he paid his dollar and challenged the man to do so.

The Guesser looked Timmy up and down like a butcher inspecting a side of beef. He squinted his eyes. He rubbed his chin, and Timmy saw dandruff fall like snowflakes from his beard. Finally The Guesser was ready.

"Eighty-five pounds!" he bellowed confidently.

Timmy grinned. "Uh-uh," he said. "I weigh seventy-eight pounds."

The Guesser's eyes opened wide with disbelief. "Step over here," he demanded.

By the shelves with the toys, The Guesser kept a small scale. He had Timmy get on it. It read 79 pounds — still six less than the man had guessed. Timmy would get his choice of toys.

There was much to pick from. A whistle. A rubber spider. A baseball card of a player Timmy had never heard of. Some paste-on tattoos. And much more.

Howard was getting impatient.

"Timmy, while you decide on a prize, I'm going to go for a ride on the Toboggan," he said. "I'll meet you over there."

That was fine with Timmy. The Toboggan was one of those rides that went round and round and made him sick to his stomach.

Timmy examined the prizes for a few minutes, until The Guesser finally stamped his feet in impatience. He finally chose a plastic bookmark with a calendar from the previous year printed on it.

Timmy left the Guesser feeling happy that he had won a prize.

Little did he know that The Guesser was happy, too — because the bookmark, like all his prizes, cost much less than the dollar Timmy had paid to play.

As he walked away, examining his prize, Timmy felt a strong hand suddenly grab his shoulder from behind.

It was Hank. It had to be.

Timmy's knees went weak, and his heart began to race with fear.

Chapter Five

"Here, kid, you forgot this."

The Guesser handed Timmy his sweater, which he had removed so the man could get a better look at his build.

Timmy breathed a sigh of relief. He was sure it had been Hank Wilson.

When he walked over to the Toboggan, Timmy found Howard still in line waiting to get on the ride. There were about twenty people ahead of Howard, so Timmy decided to go over to a nearby lemonade stand.

That scare a minute ago had left his mouth dry.

There were two lines outside the windows at the lemonade stand. Timmy joined the one on the left. A moment later, Sally and two other girls from school got in the other line.

Timmy waved a greeting to the girls. They

chatted back and forth. Timmy told them about the prize he won. The girls regaled him with stories about the rides they had ridden. Sally didn't even blush.

Finally, Timmy reached the front of his line. He plunked down his money, took a straw from the dispenser by the window and turned to walk a few feet away where he could wait to talk some more to the girls — especially Sally.

He took two steps, then felt something hard hit his ankle. He lost his balance and went sprawling. So did his lemonade, which splashed the legs of a teenaged girl standing in line with her boyfriend.

The girl screamed in shock as the lemonade hit her. Her date swore at Timmy.

From behind him, Timmy heard another voice. He shuddered.

He knew that voice instantly.

"Looks like Timid Timmy had an accident," the voice said in a mocking tone.

Still on the ground, Timmy looked behind him. Hank stood there with a cruel smile on his face. As usual, Duane and Jason were with him.

In a flash, Timmy realized what had happened. He had been so busy putting his change in his pocket after he had bought the lemonade, he hadn't even seen

Hank step up from the side, kick him in the ankle and trip him.

Timmy heard some of the people in the lemonade line laughing at him.

"Clumsy kid," somebody muttered.

"He should pay attention to what he's doing," said another.

Then Timmy's eyes met Sally's.

She quickly looked away, embarrassed for him. Her two friends gave him pitying looks, like they might give a dog that had been run over.

It was more than Timmy could bear.

He struggled to his feet, and cried out in pain. He had skinned both his knees. The raw skin on one was visible through a fresh rip in his pants.

Everything became a fog. Time seemed to stop.

Again he saw Sally, pretending something else had caught her eye. Again he saw the faces of people in the lemonade line, laughing at him. Again he saw Hank, resting his hands on his hips, daring him to do something.

Tears streaming down his face, Timmy ran.

He didn't know where he was going. He only knew he had to get away from there.

He darted back into the crowded midway. It was more packed than ever, but he kept running.

He dashed through the middle of some groups of people, and bolted around others.

As he sprinted past one of the scariest rides, the Hammer, Timmy accidentally stepped on a woman's foot.

"Hey!" she shouted angrily.

Timmy didn't stop to apologize. He continued to run blindly, bumping into people.

He fell again, ripping the other knee of his pants.

His heart was pounding like a drum. He was panting like a dog. He could scarcely catch his breath. He dragged himself off the midway, over to an area with a few games and food vendors.

He bent over, gasping, trying to get his breath. He was hot. Sweat beaded on his forehead and trickled down his back. His hair was damp.

After a couple of minutes, he could almost breathe normally. But he was still in a daze. He was about to start running again when something caught his eye.

Off in a darkened corner near the midway was a tiny cottage. Unlike everything else at the carnival, it was not well lit. Nobody outside beckoned people to come in.

Only a simple, white sign with peeling paint and faded red letters told what was inside:

"Myra the Mystic. Fortunes read. Wishes granted."

Cautiously, Timmy walked up to the door.

The curtains were closed. There were no sounds from inside, but it appeared one dim light was lit.

Something about the place made Timmy uneasy. It was spooky. But he took a deep breath and summoned up as much courage as he could muster.

Then he knocked on the door.

Chapter Six

Nobody answered.

Timmy waited a minute, then pounded harder on the door.

This time he thought he heard somebody stirring inside. Then he heard the shuffle of footsteps.

The door opened.

Standing there gazing at Timmy was a middle-aged lady with long black hair streaked with gray, a long nose and fierce black eyes that burned like lumps of coal.

She wore a long, flowing dress with a sash for a belt. Her toes peeked out from her sandals. She had a colorful scarf in her hair.

She was, thought Timmy, the most unusual looking person he had ever seen.

"What do you want?" the woman asked hoarsely.

The woman scared Timmy. He had to fight an urge to run.

"The sign says you grant wishes," Timmy stammered. "I want you to grant me a wish."

Timmy couldn't believe what he had just said. His mother had once told him that fortune telling, reading people's minds, granting wishes and casting spells was all make believe. Nobody could really do these things.

Yet here he was, asking a strange woman at a carnival to grant him a wish.

He thought again about running, but then the woman spoke.

"Wishes are powerful things," she said. "They cost more money than a boy like you has. Just how much money do you have?"

Timmy fumbled through his jeans pockets and produced several crumpled bills, a few coins and some lint.

Nervously, he added it up.

"I have $15.75," he said hopefully. It was every cent he had saved in the past few weeks.

"And I'll give you this bookmark," he added, removing the prize he had won from The Guesser from a shirt pocket.

"I'm sorry, you don't have enough money," the woman said, starting to close the door.

"Please!" Timmy wailed. "This is really important to me!"

The woman paused and looked Timmy over from head to foot. She seemed to notice for the first time the sweat stains on his shirt and the rips in his pants.

"I'll grant you one wish," the woman said reluctantly. "I am Myra. Come inside."

Timmy entered a small, murky room lit only by a small lamp in one corner. Much of the room was taken up by a table with one chair on each side of it.

Myra the Mystic plopped down in one of these chairs. She motioned toward the other seat.

"Sit!" she commanded.

The mysterious woman then took Timmy's $15.75. She let him keep his bookmark.

Timmy looked around the room. A ceramic cow with wings hung from the ceiling. A skull was nailed to one wall. Beneath it, on top of a small cabinet, a candle flickered. The fluttering light made the skull seem like it was grinning.

It cast an eerie shadow on the wall.

Beyond this room, Timmy guessed there were

25

at least two more rooms. Colorful glass beads hung from the doorway leading to these other rooms, and Timmy could not see through them.

At the table where he now sat were a dozen bottles. Some were green, others blue and red and yellow. Inside were various liquids Timmy could not recognize. Next to the bottles sat two decks of cards.

"Now, what is the wish you want granted?" Myra asked.

Timmy looked at her again. She was staring at him. It felt as if her eyes were boring right through him.

Don't chicken out now, Timmy said to himself.

Then he answered Myra the Mystic.

"I want to be strong," he whispered. "Stronger than any other boy in my class."

Chapter Seven

"I can make you strong," Myra assured Timmy. "But you might find you don't like being strong. Perhaps it will do you more bad than good. Think carefully about this decision."

Timmy didn't need to think about it. If he were strong, he could stand up to Hank and his friends. He would show them!

"I want to be strong," he repeated.

Without another word, the woman opened one of the bottles on the table. She poured its milky contents into her hands and rubbed them together.

Then she poured some more of the goop into her hands and reached for Timmy's face.

He tried to back away. Too late.

Myra rubbed the stuff all over his face. It felt hot and seemed to penetrate every pore in his skin. At first he made a face and he struggled.

"Be still!" Myra barked. Timmy was still.

When she finished, Myra grabbed Timmy's hands and gripped them tightly in hers. She closed her eyes and began mumbling in a language Timmy had never heard.

Timmy watched her in amazement. But he felt awkward. It was like keeping your eyes open in church when everybody else's were closed during a prayer. So Timmy closed his eyes too.

A minute later, it was over. Myra released Timmy's hands. They were red from being squeezed so hard.

"That's it?" he asked. "That's all?"

"That is all," Myra replied. "Now you will be strong."

"But I don't feel any different," Timmy protested. "I don't think it worked."

Myra shook her head impatiently. "These things take time. You will see. The spell will work."

Timmy didn't believe her.

"I'm not leaving here until I am strong," he said, surprised at how brave he sounded. "Either that, or give me back my money!"

Suddenly, Timmy felt a stab of pain in his right leg.

"Owww!" he shrieked.

He bolted out of his chair, knocking over the table with all of Myra the Mystic's bottles of potions.

Chapter Eight

Timmy looked down at his throbbing leg. A black cat was digging its claws into him, using his leg as a scratching post.

"You fool!" Myra screamed at Timmy, as she scrambled to scoop up the bottles scattered across the floor. Odd-looking ointments and potions oozed from most of them.

Then Myra turned her attention to the cat.

"Bootsy, come here," she called in a softer voice. The cat let go of Timmy and sauntered over to Myra.

"I'm sorry," Timmy sputtered. "Let me help you pick up the bottles.

Myra would have none of it. She was already pushing Timmy toward the door.

"Leave!" she commanded.

Timmy stumbled outside, back into the brightly

lit world of the carnival. He felt stupid. First, Hank had made a fool of him at the lemonade stand. Now this woman had taken all his money, and he still wasn't strong.

He wandered aimlessly. He had no money, so he couldn't play any of the carnival games, or buy anything to eat or drink.

But he was in no hurry to go home. His mother would be upset when she saw the rips in his jeans or, worse, learned he had spent all his money.

Timmy walked by the animal freak show and saw a small crowd gathered in front of the ticket booth. Most were high school kids on dates, debating whether or not to buy tickets.

A man with a microphone was doing his best to help them decide.

"Freaks of nature like you've never seen!" he hollered. "See the two-headed calf. Or how about the lamb with five legs? And we have a snake born without eyes! All of them alive, ladies and gentlemen! Come, take a look!"

Stretched overhead between poles were canvases with cartoonish drawings of the animals inside. The sideshow even claimed to have a unicorn on display.

31

"I wonder if they're real," a girl of about 16 murmured to the boy she was with. They decided to find out. They bought tickets and went inside. So did half of the other people outside the sideshow.

Even if he hadn't given all his money to Myra the Mystic, Timmy wasn't sure he would pay to see the animals. He was curious about how they looked. But paying money to gawk at the unfortunate beasts didn't seem right.

He continued to walk along the midway. Shrieks of laughter and fear pierced the air when he passed the fastest rides. The smell of popcorn and cotton candy was everywhere.

Timmy felt sad. He wished he hadn't spent all his money. He wished he could buy a corn dog and a lemonade. He wished he could buy a ticket to a ride or an exhibit.

Suddenly tired, he found a bench and sat down.

"I made a mess of things at the carnival again," he muttered to himself. "Just like last year."

Then something strange happened. At first Timmy thought he imagined it.

He began getting a tingly feeling in his body. It started in his chest. Then it moved to his shoulders.

Finally, his arms. The sensation kept growing stronger, more intense.

Timmy thought he could actually feel his muscles getting bigger. He thought they might pop right out of his skin.

He looked at his arms. They were as puny as ever. He made a muscle. No change there, either.

But Timmy was certain something was different. Maybe he *was* stronger. Maybe the mystic's spell had worked after all!

He decided he had to find out.

Chapter Nine

Earlier, when he had visited Myra the Mystic, Timmy had noticed a carny struggling to change a flat tire on his car in the darkened dirt parking lot beyond the midway. The man was having trouble because his jack kept falling over in the soft soil.

Now Timmy went back there. Sure enough, the carny was still trying to jack up the car. As Timmy drew nearer, he saw the car was up in the air. Just then, the jack quivered and tumbled, and the car hit the dirt with a thud.

The carny cursed loudly and threw his baseball cap to the ground in disgust.

"Excuse me," Timmy said.

The carny looked startled. He had not heard Timmy approach.

"What do you want?" he asked angrily.

The man was wearing a soiled tank top and

grimy jeans. He had a gritty face and greasy hair. He was sweating a lot . He had a tattoo of a dragon on his left arm and one of a pirate on his right arm. He was missing two teeth. His remaining molars were crooked and yellow.

"I'd like to help you with that tire," Timmy said. "I think I can hold your car up while you change it."

"A little squirt like you? Yeah, sure kid. If you can do that, I'm the president of the United States. Scram!"

Instead of leaving, Timmy rushed over to the man's car. It was an old model with dings and dents. Like the carny, it was covered with dust.

Timmy squared himself in front of the heap and lifted with all his might.

The car raised up off the ground, one foot, two feet, then three feet. Then Timmy set it down.

The carny stood with his mouth open and his eyes wide with disbelief.

"How did you do that? Is that some sort of trick?

"No, sir. I'm just strong," Timmy replied proudly.

The truth was, he was as astonished as the

35

carny. He hadn't wasted his money after all! Myra the Mystic's spell was working! He had never imagined he would be this strong!

"Now, would you like me to help you change that tire?" Timmy asked.

"You bet!"

Again, Timmy lifted the man's car. The carny removed the flat tire. He placed the spare on, and then Timmy asked for a short rest.

After a couple of more minutes, Timmy picked up the front of the car again, and the carny tightened the lug nuts on the spare. At last, the job was finished.

"You're an amazing kid," the carny said, scratching his head. "You work in one of the shows here?"

"No, I live in this town," Timmy said. "I don't travel with the carnival."

"I bet I could get you a job here," the carny said. "People would pay to see you lift heavy things."

"No thanks," Timmy replied. "I've got to finish school. I don't think my parents would like me traveling with a carnival."

Still, he was flattered by the offer.

"Well, then, at least take this," the carny said. He dug through his pockets and produced a $5 bill.

"That's for helping me," the man said gratefully. "Thanks."

"You're welcome, Mr. President," Timmy replied.

"Huh?"

"You said if I could lift your car, then you were the president of the United States," Timmy said.

He headed back to the midway. He knew exactly what he wanted to do next.

Find Hank Wilson.

Chapter Ten

Back on the midway, Timmy began looking for Hank.

He no longer was tired. In fact, he had so much energy, he could hardly contain himself.

Even though he was anxious to find Hank, Timmy stopped to buy a ticket to see the two-headed woman.

He walked inside the trailer and sat in one of the metal folding chairs facing a tiny stage. The show was to start in five minutes. Four other people also were seated.

Then the curtain opened on the little stage and a spotlight shone on the two-headed woman. She was standing behind a railing on the stage. To the rear of the stage was a sofa in case she got tired and wanted to sit.

Timmy immediately regretted buying a ticket.

It was clear to him that the two-headed woman was actually two women inside one very large dress.

Both were about twenty-one years old. They did not look at all alike.

"Good evening," one head greeted the small audience.

"We're so glad you could visit," chirped the other head.

The woman said her name was Martha. The doctors hadn't expected her to live long after she was born this way, but she had fooled them. Kids at school had made fun of her, she said, and dating had been a problem.

"Sometimes a boy doesn't know whether to kiss me," said the first head.

"Or me," piped up the other.

Meals were also a challenge, the two-headed woman said.

"I like hot dogs with sauerkraut," said the first head, smiling at the thought.

"But I hate sauerkraut and love meat loaf," said the second head.

"Ugh, I don't like meat loaf," said the first head, wrinkling up her nose.

When her mother made a meal that one head

39

didn't like, she would also prepare a second course to make the other head happy, Martha said.

She spoke a little longer, then sang a tune that ended the show. Timmy thought the second head had a nicer voice than the first. He walked out of the trailer feeling cheated out of his money.

Back on the midway, he resumed his search for Hank. He smiled as he thought about the surprise Hank and his friends were about to get. He would get even with them for bullying him.

He couldn't wait to see the expression on Hank's face when he found out Timmy was now stronger than he was.

It didn't take Timmy long to find his tormentors.

They were seated at Water Race, a game in which players shoot water pistols at cylinders which advance toy horses in a race. The first player to fill his target with water has his horse cross the finish line and wins a small prize.

Hank, Duane and Jason all had their backs to Timmy as he walked up to them. A new race was about to begin. The man running the game talked a blue streak, trying to get more people to join the race. At least a dozen were already in the race.

Then a bell rang like the one at a real race track.

"And they're off!" the game operator bellowed.

Hank had a horse named Fantastic Phillie, which quickly took the lead. Timmy noticed that Hank had already won three small prizes, which he would be able to trade in for a larger gift.

"It's Fantastic Phillie in the lead, Mama Mia running second and Jubilee in third," intoned the game operator.

As the race continued, Hank's horse seemed to be widening its lead over the others.

Timmy decided to strike.

Chapter Eleven

Just as Hank's horse neared the finish line, Timmy came up close behind the bully.

Hank was so intent at shooting water at the target, he didn't see Timmy.

Timmy reached over and grabbed the hand in which Hank held the water pistol. Then he squeezed Hank's hand. Hard.

"Owwww!" Hank screamed.

Timmy looked at Hank's face. Instead of his usual scowl, or smirk, he looked startled and scared. And maybe amazed at who had his hand in this vice grip.

He tried to free his hand from Timmy's. He couldn't.

Meanwhile, he had stopped aiming at the target and the stream of water from his pistol was hitting the game's operator squarely in the face.

The man began yelling. Timmy couldn't tell if he was angry at him or Hank. He didn't wait to find out.

He took off down the midway, but not too fast. He wanted Hank and his pals to keep him in sight.

As soon as Timmy let go of his hand, Hank jumped up from his stool, knocking the prizes he had won to the ground.

"Come on you guys!" he shouted to Duane and Jason. "Let's get him!"

All three sped off in pursuit of Timmy.

A few yards ahead, Timmy jogged through the crowd. He kept looking over his shoulder to be sure Hank and the others were not losing sight of him.

Then he veered off to the right and raced behind the Haunted House. It was dark here. He stopped as soon as he was behind the place.

With one shoulder against the Haunted House, Timmy peeked around at the midway. His pursuers would be here any moment. His chest heaved from running and he gulped air.

He watched and waited.

Timmy could hear thumping sounds coming from inside the Haunted House. Every few seconds, there were screams. In the past this would have scared Timmy. But not tonight. Instead, he felt like he could conquer anything. He had never felt this way before, and he liked it.

Suddenly Hank and the others came running around the corner in Timmy's direction. As Timmy had hoped, Hank was the nearest to him.

Timmy crouched, waiting.

As Hank ran past, Timmy leaped out of the shadows and tackled him.

Hank let out a surprised cry. He hit the ground with a thud.

Timmy pounced on him, pinning one arm behind his back.

Duane and Jason had turned back and were now coming toward Timmy and Hank.

"Help me!" Hank called.

Timmy grabbed Hank by his shirt collar and the seat of his pants. He lifted him over his head, and held him aloft like a doll.

Hank started whimpering like a puppy.

"Don't drop me, Timmy. Please!"

Duane and Jason stopped in their tracks. Their jaws dropped, and they stared in disbelief. Both boys were confused. They were trying to figure out how

Timmy had hoisted Hank in the air. And they were wondering what they could do about it.

"Stay right there," Timmy barked at them. He was startled at how fierce he sounded.

"Don't come any closer, or I'll drop him. And then I'll do the same to each of you."

Duane and Jason backed up a couple of steps. They just stood there, not sure what to do next.

"Let me down," blubbered Hank. The voice of the bully now sounded like that of a small, frightened child.

"Not until you apologize for everything you've done to me," Timmy replied. "Ooh, my arms are getting tired," he fibbed, pretending to lose his grip.

"I'm sorry! I'm sorry for everything," Hank cried nervously. "Now *please* put me down!"

Timmy lowered Hank to the ground. Hank was shaking and rubbing the hand that Timmy had squeezed at the horse race game. It was red and sore.

"What happened to you?" Hank asked. "How did you get so strong?"

"It doesn't matter," Timmy replied. "The important thing is, you guys are going to leave me alone after this, okay?"

"Okay!" Hank, Duane and Jason cried in unison.

"Now scram!" Timmy demanded.

All three boys ran away, as fast as if they were fleeing a ghost.

Chapter Twelve

Timmy remained behind the Haunted House a minute longer, thinking about what had just happened.

He would no longer be bothered by Hank and his friends.

At last, he would be able to walk around school without looking over his shoulder to see if they were following him. Now he could walk to and from school and know that they could not take his money from him.

Timmy not only felt stronger, he also felt more aggressive. He wasn't going to be picked on by *anybody*. The money he had given Myra the Mystic had been well-spent, he thought to himself. He could not have been happier.

He walked back to the midway. He had a swagger in his stride and a bounce in his step.

He walked past the House of Mirrors and the

Tilt-A-Whirl. As he approached the Ferris wheel, he saw Howard, Sally and her two friends getting off of it.

He walked up to them.

"Where have you been?" Howard asked. "I looked everywhere for you."

Timmy quickly told him about Myra the Mystic and the spell that made him strong.

"I even scared Hank and Duane and Jason," he said excitedly. "They won't be bothering me again!"

Howard shook his head. "You don't have to make up stories. I heard what happened at the lemonade stand."

"No, really," Timmy insisted. "I'll prove it to you."

At Timmy's insistence, Howard and the girls went with him a little further down the midway to the Hi-Striker. It was a mainstay at every carnival.

The player paid to take a mallet and slam it down on a certain spot. This would send a metal disc up a long, wire track. The strongest players would propel the disc all the way to the top, where it would ring a bell. Winners got a cheap cigar.

The Hi-Striker was a popular game for young men trying to show off for their dates. As Timmy and his friends walked up, there was a big crowd watching as a muscular man prepared to take a swing.

The man was about twenty-two years old. He wore a tank top that showed off his massive arms and shoulders. He winked at the pretty blonde who was his date. He rubbed his hands together and picked up the mallet.

He had the confident look of a man about to win a prize.

He lifted the mallet over his head, then brought it down with a mighty swing, emitting a loud grunt.

The disc traveled up the incline, but only three-quarters of the way to the top, to a spot that read, "Cream Puff." The crowd groaned. The man looked angry as he walked away. His girlfriend tried to console him, telling him the game wasn't important.

"Who wants to try next?" called out the fellow who operated the Hi-Striker. "Who's strong enough to ring the bell? Come on up here, guys."

Several young men who had taken their money out, planning to take a swing, now hung back in the crowd. When the guy with the big muscles failed to ring the bell, they figured they probably would come up short, too.

"Come on, let's have a player!" the carny

challenged. "Aren't there any strong guys here?"

"I'll try it," Timmy called out. He made his way through the spectators.

"What's he doing?" Sally whispered to Howard. "He's going to make a fool of himself."

"I know," Howard said with a sigh. "He's acting very strangely."

A ripple of laughter swept through the spectators when they saw Timmy pay his dollar. He could hear their comments.

"This ought to be pretty funny."

"The mallet's as big as him."

"This kid must be crazy."

The game operator seemed reluctant to take Timmy's money. He was afraid this skinny little kid would hurt himself. But nobody else volunteered, so he relented.

The mallet was in fact nearly as big as Timmy.

But when he picked it up, it felt light. He eyed the spot he had to hit, brought the mallet over his head, then brought it down with all his might.

When the mallet hit the platform, there was a resounding crack, like that of a bat hitting a baseball a very long way. The disc flew up the incline so fast that nobody actually saw it. It then smashed the bell with such incredible force that the bell and disc both soared a hundred feet into the air.

For a moment, there was silence, except for the sounds of nearby rides.

None of the spectators could believe what they had seen. Neither could the game operator.

And neither, for that matter, could Timmy.

Everybody just stared in disbelief at the spot where the bell had been moments before.

Then the crowd erupted in applause. People started slapping Timmy on the back and shaking his hand.

"Way to go, kid!"

"Amazing! Are you for real?"

The game operator would have to shut down the Hi-Striker until he found somebody to fix the bell. But he wasn't angry.

"In twenty-five years of running this game, I've never had that happen," he told Timmy. "Especially not by a kid."

Since Timmy was too young to smoke, the game operator couldn't give him a cigar. So he gave him his dollar back.

"Do me a favor, kid," he said. "Don't play my game again."

The crowd around the Hi-Striker began to fan out.

Howard and Sally were still there. They were looking at Timmy in a way they had never looked at him before.

Chapter Thirteen

"Now do you believe me about Myra the Mystic?" Timmy asked Howard.

"I believe you. Man, that was really something!"

"Well, don't tell anybody how I became strong," Timmy said. "If everybody knows, maybe they'll pay Myra to make them strong. And if that happens, I won't be the strongest boy in class."

Timmy, Howard, Sally and her friends went on a couple of rides together. By then it was almost 10 o'clock and Timmy had to go home. So did most of the others.

Sally's mother came to pick up her and her friends and drive them home.

"Gee, Timmy, I never knew you were so strong," Sally said as she was leaving. "Let's eat lunch together at school on Monday."

Timmy walked with Howard to his house, then went the rest of the way home alone.

As he approached his front door, he was worried. If his mother saw he had ripped his pants, she would be very angry. He opened the door as quietly as he could and went inside.

He could hear his mother puttering around in the kitchen. The television was on in the living room. That's probably where his father was.

Timmy tiptoed down the hall to his bedroom and closed the door. He changed his pants. He looked in the mirror and saw his shirt was dirty, so he got out a clean one.

Before he put on the clean shirt, he looked closely at himself in the mirror. His arms and chest looked the same as always. Small.

Did he really have super strength, or was what happened earlier a dream?

Timmy began to wonder. It seemed too incredible to be true.

Maybe he didn't dream it, but perhaps the spell was over. Myra never said how long his strength would last. He had just assumed it was forever.

But what if it already was gone?

He had to find out. But how?

He looked around his room for a way to test his strength. The dresser was too wide to get his arms around. His bed was too long. But in a corner of the room was a cigar store Indian his parents had bought a few years ago at an antique store.

His parents used to keep the Indian in the den. But it became too crowded in that room. Timmy had always liked the Indian, so he had asked if he could keep it in his room.

The Indian was more than six feet tall and carved from a solid, heavy block of wood. It must have weighed at least three hundred pounds. Once, Timmy had tried to slide the Indian along the floor because he wanted it in a different corner of the room. He couldn't move it.

Now, he decided, he would try to lift the statue in the air. Just like he had done with Hank earlier tonight.

Timmy grinned at the memory of Hank squirming helplessly as he was hoisted in the air.

Timmy bent low so he could wrap his arms around the Indian's legs. Then he stood up, lifting the Indian. He struggled to maneuver his hands in a way so that he could get the Indian in the air. It was hard, not because of the Indian's weight, but because of his height.

Finally, Timmy succeeded in raising the statue straight up in the air. As he did so, the Indian's head hit the ceiling with a loud thump.

Timmy began to lower the Indian back to the floor when he heard footsteps coming toward his room. He froze, with the Indian still in the air.

He knew the sound of those steps. His mother was coming.

Chapter Fourteen

"Timmy, are you in there?"

"Just a minute, Mom. I'm changing my clothes."

Timmy's parents always knocked on the door or called his name before entering his room. Timmy was glad they respected his privacy — and never more glad than he was right now.

As quickly and quietly as he could, Timmy set the Indian back in its place in the corner. Then he opened his bedroom door.

His mother stood there, looking puzzled.

"When did you get home?" she asked. She seemed a little irritated.

"Just a minute ago. I was about to come out and tell you."

"Well, it's five minutes after ten. Your father and I were getting ready to drive over to the carnival and look for you."

Timmy's mother glanced around his room, seeing if anything was out of place. "What was that noise I heard in here?"

"I, um, was moving my bed to look for a book I lost."

Timmy hated to lie, and seldom did. But this was one of those times when he felt he had to.

Timmy's mother looked him over suspiciously to see if anything was amiss.

After a minute, she seemed satisfied.

"Did you have fun at the carnival, Timmy?"

"Yes, I had a good time."

"Did you spend all your money?"

"Uh-uh." Timmy shook his head.

He showed his mother the money he brought home. Of course, she had no way of knowing that he had been given that money for holding the carny's car off the ground while he changed a tire.

"Well, good, you know how important it is to save some of your money."

Timmy decided not to tell his parents about Myra the Mystic, his sudden strength or his eye-popping feat at the Hi-Striker. They wouldn't believe him. And if he proved it by demonstrating how strong he was, it probably would scare them silly to know that their son had this power.

"So, there was nothing unusual this year at the carnival?" Timmy's mother asked.

Timmy wondered if she could read his mind. Or had already heard something. He decided to stick to his story. He didn't want to worry her.

"No, Mom," he said. "It was just like any other carnival."

Chapter Fifteen

It was a typical weekend for Timmy.

He did chores around the house, hung out with Howard and worked on a book report for school.

He did not test his strength again.

Come Monday morning, Timmy couldn't wait to get back to school. Now he would be able to hold his own outside the classroom as well as inside it.

When he arrived at school, Timmy quickly learned that most of his classmates had heard about his display of power on the Hi-Striker Friday night. Several kids who normally said little to him, greeted him and asked if the story was true.

Timmy enjoyed being the center of attention. It was a new experience for him. Even after class began, it seemed like some of his classmates were watching him with new interest. In the past, he might as well have been invisible.

Timmy ate lunch with Sally, but several other kids joined them and continued to ask Timmy questions about his feat at the carnival.

After lunch, most of the boys and a few of the girls headed to the schoolyard to start a softball game before class resumed. Timmy hadn't planned on playing, but several boys insisted that he join them.

Hank and a boy named Willie were picking the teams. Hank chose first. He immediately selected Timmy. The same Timmy who was always picked last. The same Timmy who never hit the ball out of the infield.

Timmy couldn't believe it. He felt like a big shot.

Timmy figured that Hank picked him for two reasons. Since he was now so strong, Hank hoped he would hit a couple of home runs for his team. But Timmy also thought maybe it was Hank's way of thanking him for not telling the kids at school that he had held Hank in the air and made him beg for mercy.

Timmy had told only Howard about the incident. And since Howard hadn't seen it, he did not mention it. The truth was, Howard still was not sure he believed the story.

Being the weakest hitter, Timmy usually batted

last in softball games. But today, Hank told him to bat third.

He came to bat in the first inning with a runner on first base and one out. This would be his first chance to show the entire class the new Timmy. The strong Timmy.

The first pitch came in a high arc. It looked as easy to swat as a melon.

Timmy swung mightily and missed. He waved at the next pitch, and missed it too. The pitcher struck him out on the third pitch.

Timmy realized then that being strong wouldn't automatically make him a better player. He would be as bad as ever if he couldn't make contact with the ball. He felt like the same old klutz who nobody wanted on their team.

"You'll hit one next time," Hank said encouragingly.

It didn't take long for Timmy to get another chance. In the second inning it was his turn to bat again. There were runners on every base and two outs. His team was losing by two runs.

Before Timmy walked to the plate, Hank offered some advice.

"Don't swing so hard. If you swing easier, you

won't move your head and you'll be able to keep your eye on the pitch. With your power, you don't need to swing hard to give it a good ride."

Timmy stepped up to the plate and waited. The first pitch came in fat and tempting. He swung and missed.

The next pitch, the same thing again.

"Come on Timmy. Just meet the ball," Hank shouted.

Moments later, the next pitch was on its way. Timmy swung, nice and easy.

This time he connected.

The ball disappeared with a whoosh, like it had been shot out of a cannon. It soared so high, so fast, that few of the players even saw it.

Those who did hollered in disbelief.

"No way! That can't be!" yelled the pitcher.

He stood looking up in the air toward center field as if he were watching a missile that had just been launched.

The ball kept carrying. It sailed beyond the field on which Timmy and his classmates were playing. It continued over the playing field beyond. It finally landed over a tall chain-link fence that encircled the schoolyard.

Nobody had ever hit a ball anywhere near that far before. No child. No adult.

Timmy circled the bases and crossed home plate. He had hit a grand slam home run. He had given his team the lead. His teammates slapped him on the back and gave him high fives.

No one had ever given Timmy a high five before. He kind of liked it.

But now there was a problem. The game could not go on until they recovered the ball. Several of the boys ran to the fence the ball had gone over. Hank said he would climb the fence and retrieve it.

But when the boys reached the fence, they saw there was no use in trying. They could see the ball had landed on the other side of a swampy creek that flowed behind the schoolyard. It would be too dangerous for anybody to wade into the snake-infested creek to go after the ball.

The boys headed back to the baseball diamond. With no ball, everybody just stood around marveling at Timmy's hit.

"Way to go, Timmy!" said a boy Timmy hardly knew.

"Next time, I want you on my team," said Willie, the captain of the other team.

"Not if I can help it," Hank retorted.

Timmy was enjoying the adulation.

But not for long.

"Timmy!" a voice called out crossly.

Timmy turned to see Mr. Halpern, the principal, striding toward him. Mr. Halpern did not look happy.

"I want to see you in my office in five minutes!" the principal said.

Then, turning his back, he strode angrily away.

Chapter Sixteen

When Timmy entered Mr. Halpern's office, he knew he was in trouble. He just didn't know why.

The principal was pacing around his desk. He had white hair and a red face that always looked sunburned. He wore a brown suit with a white shirt. On his desk were photographs of his wife, children and grandchildren.

"I understand you lost school property today. Namely a softball," said Mr. Halpern, peering sternly at Timmy over thick black eyeglasses.

"Sort of."

"Tell me what happened."

"I hit it over the fence. I didn't mean to," said Timmy, feeling a mixture of embarrassment and pride.

"Yes, yes, that's what some of the other children told me. I don't know why they are covering up for you, Timmy. We both know that's not true. A grown man couldn't hit the ball that far, much less a small boy like you. Now, what really happened?"

"That *is* what happened," Timmy insisted.

"Very well. If you persist in lying to me, you will have to stay after school. Report to my office as soon as school is out. I'm very disappointed in you, Timmy. This isn't like you."

Mr. Halpern watched Timmy to see if the threat of being kept after school would loosen his tongue. It didn't.

Timmy could have proved he was telling the truth by demonstrating his super strength for Mr. Halpern. But he didn't dare. He was afraid that would get him in more trouble.

He guessed the school would tell his parents. They would want to know how he became so strong. Then they would go back to the carnival with him and make Myra the Mystic lift the spell.

Timmy didn't want that.

It was fun being the center of attention. He liked the way his classmates were so interested in him. So he said nothing.

Mr. Halpern told him to return to his class. When school let out, everybody in Timmy's class headed home, or to the arcade, Little League practice or a Girl Scout meeting.

Everybody but Timmy.

Timmy trudged down the hall to the principal's office. He opened the door and went in.

"Oh no," he groaned.

Chapter Seventeen

Waiting inside Mr. Halpern's office was the school janitor, Mr. King. Timmy knew what was coming next.

"You'll be helping Mr. King clean classrooms and bathrooms for two hours today," said Mr. Halpern, a thin smile flickering across his lips. "You can start right now."

Timmy followed Mr. King to his small office. It had no windows and was stuffy and smelled of chemicals.

There was a tiny, battered desk in the room. The rest of the room was cluttered with brooms, mops, buckets, paper towels and cleaning solvents.

Mr. King explained to Timmy what they would be doing. They would start off cleaning bathrooms. Then, if time permitted, Timmy would help tidy up the classrooms. Mr. King would work with Timmy to make sure he did the job right.

In the bathrooms, Timmy scrubbed toilets, swept and mopped floors and cleaned mirrors. Mr. King did some of this too, but he also did lighter work such as refilling paper towel and toilet paper dispensers.

Timmy was interested in seeing the girls' bathrooms. He was disappointed to find they didn't look much different than those for the boys. And he was surprised to see the girls were just as messy as the boys.

Cleaning bathrooms was hard work, and Timmy couldn't wait to be done. Finally, he and Mr. King moved on to the classrooms.

There, they emptied waste baskets, swept floors and scraped gunk off desks, and from under them. The gunk included gum, candy and glue.

This was hard work, too. Timmy scraped two knuckles raw while he scrubbed beneath desks. He bumped his head on a desk when he raised up quickly from cleaning below it. And his back was getting sore from bending and twisting to reach spots in need of cleaning.

Timmy had never given Mr. King much thought, good or bad. After seeing how hard his job was, he had new respect for the man.

Timmy was just finishing his second classroom when Mr. Halpern stuck his red face in the door.

"It's been two hours, Timmy. You can go home."

As Timmy gathered his things, Mr. Halpern left him with a warning. "If this happens again, we'll have to call your parents."

When Timmy got home, he found his mother in the kitchen making dinner. It smelled like fish.

"Why so late today?" she asked.

"I stopped at the arcade with Howard."

"But Howard came here an hour ago looking for you." Timmy's mother was looking at him suspiciously now.

Timmy was ashamed of himself. Again, he had told his mother a lie. And this time, he had gotten caught.

"Uh, Howard left the arcade earlier than me. I guess he thought I was leaving right after him."

Timmy didn't think he sounded very convincing. His mother didn't either. But before she could ask him another question, a pan of water boiling on the stove began to hiss and overflow.

"Uh-oh," said Timmy's mother. As she

reached for a pot holder, Timmy quietly left the kitchen and went to his room.

Later at dinner, Timmy's mother seemed to have forgotten about his coming home late from school. It was a good thing, because Timmy didn't know what he would tell her if she asked more questions.

That night, Timmy had a hard time focusing on his homework. He was fretting about how his new power had gotten him in trouble at school.

The day had begun so full of promise and ended so badly. He hoped tomorrow would be better.

But he had a terrible feeling it would be worse.

Chapter Eighteen

The next day at school, Timmy was the center of attention again.

Many of his classmates asked him about having to stay after school. In their eyes, he had become the bad boy, the misfit of the classroom — a reputation previously reserved for Hank and his pals.

"Gee, Timmy, I never thought *you* would have to stay after school," Howard said, shaking his head in disbelief.

"It wasn't even my fault," said Timmy miserably. "I didn't mean to hit the ball out of the school yard. It just happened."

After lunch, many of the kids played softball again. Several of them begged Timmy to join them. Everybody wanted to be on Timmy's team.

Timmy said no. He wasn't about to get in trouble again if he could help it. He kept remembering

Mr. Halpern's threat to call his parents if something happened again.

The rest of the day, Timmy tried not to draw attention to himself and his strength. He was relieved when school got out and he was free to go home.

"Want to stop at the arcade?" Howard asked.

Timmy thought about it a moment.

What could go wrong there? Nothing, he decided.

"Okay," he replied. "Let's go."

The arcade already was crowded with other kids when Timmy and Howard arrived.

Timmy loved the arcade. He liked the way it was dark inside, with the only light coming from the colorful games. In a way, it was like being in a movie theater, but better. In an arcade, you didn't have to keep your voice down.

In fact, the chatter among the game-players was one of the things Timmy loved.

"Nice shot. Way to go!"

"Oh no! I should have made that."

He also loved the sounds of the games themselves — the gunshots fired from imaginary weapons, the grunts and smacks from karate chops from action heroes.

"Oomp! Unhhh! Owww! Pow pow pow!"

And from speakers throughout the arcade came the pulsating sounds of rap and disco music.

Timmy and Howard bought their tokens. They decided to play Street Fighter, a game in which karate experts go one on one. Howard won the first match. Timmy took the second.

After that, the boys decided to test their mettle against the Bicep Buster.

The Bicep Buster was simple. The player grabbed a vertical grip and pushed it over and downward as far as he could. It was hard, because the grip sat atop a metal lever that barely budged. At the base of the lever was a black rubber cushion similar to that at the bottom of a car's gear shift.

The game was supposed to be like arm wrestling, with the machine rather than a human as the opponent.

The Bicep Buster, like other games at the arcade, had eye-catching pictures. It featured two shirtless men engaged in a ferocious arm-wrestling match. Two young women in skimpy dresses watched them do battle.

Above these figures in a bright yellow light, was a bulging bicep with an electrical charge coming off it.

The best score possible in the game was nine hundred ninety-nine points. The game board said that the high score so far was five hundred and six.

"You go first," Timmy urged Howard.

Howard knew his friend would cream him at this game, now that he had super strength. But he was a good sport and didn't complain.

Howard inserted his tokens and pushed against the Bicep Buster with all his might. His face turned red from trying so hard, but he only moved the grip about two inches. He got 90 points.

Next, Timmy stepped up.

He deposited his tokens and waited for the game board to clear Howard's score and start over. Then he pushed the Bicep Buster as hard as he could.

The next sound was that of Timmy and Howard gasping in dismay.

Chapter Nineteen

The grip on the Bicep Buster smashed down against the game console with a loud thunk.

It had taken Timmy less than a second to slam down his imaginary arm wrestling rival. The grip hung limply on the machine like a broken arm.

As Timmy and Howard watched in amazement, the game's point board began spinning crazily. One hundred points, two hundred, three hundred — higher and higher, and faster and faster the numbers flew by.

Nobody had ever bested the Bicep Buster. The game was not programmed for such a feat.

When the point board hit nine hundred ninety-nine — the maximum score — the numbers kept twirling madly. The machine made a horrible grinding noise. Then it hissed and sizzled. The smell of burnt wiring rose into the air.

Smoke began pouring from the game.

The owner of the arcade, Mr. Morales, ran up to Timmy and Howard.

"What's going on here?" he yelled angrily.

The boys were frozen with fear.

Mr. Morales looked at the Bicep Buster and saw that it was ruined.

"Which one of you boys destroyed my machine?" he demanded.

His face was red. Spit flew from his mouth. His hands trembled with rage.

"It was me," Timmy volunteered meekly. "I didn't mean to. I played the game, and when I beat the Bicep Buster, it broke."

"Come off it, kid. Don't you lie to me, son. You didn't beat the Bicep Buster. Even a weightlifter couldn't do that. I don't know how, but you ruined my game! And I promise you, you little twerp, somebody's going to have to pay for it!"

By now, most of the kids in the arcade had gathered around the boys and Mr. Morales, hanging on every word.

Timmy's reputation as a troublemaker would grow even more now. Timmy could just imagine the talk at school tomorrow. It made this whole terrible incident even more upsetting.

"I want you out of my arcade!" Mr. Morales hissed at Timmy, pointing a stubby finger into the boy's face. "And don't you ever come back! Do you hear me?"

But before Mr. Morales banished Timmy, he demanded Timmy's telephone number.

As Timmy watched with a sinking feeling in his stomach, the man dialed the number. After the second ring, Timmy's mother picked up the phone.

"Your son has destroyed one of my games," Mr. Morales said. "I expect you to pay for a new machine. I will send you the bill."

Mr. Morales listened to something Timmy's mother said. Then he handed the telephone to Timmy.

"She wants to talk to you."

Reluctantly, Timmy took the phone.

"Hi, Mom," he said. He tried to sound cheerful, but failed.

"Timmy you come home right now!"

His mother sounded almost as mad as Mr. Morales.

Chapter Twenty

Howard was waiting for Timmy when he left the arcade.

"I'm really in trouble now," Timmy moaned. "I'll bet a new Biceps Buster costs hundreds of dollars. Maybe thousands. And Mr. Morales is going to make my parents buy him a new one."

"What are you going to do?"

"I don't know. But I'm beginning to think that paying Myra the Mystic for super strength wasn't such a hot idea."

Timmy trudged up the walkway to his front door. A feeling of dread lay in his stomach like a bad meal. His father's car was in the driveway.

It would have been bad enough trying to explain what happened to his mother, but answering to both parents would be unbearable.

"I'm home," Timmy called out as he closed the

door behind him.

"Come in here, Timmy," his mother called from the dining room.

His mother and father were seated at the dining room table. They looked grim.

"Sit down, son," his father commanded.

His voice left no room for argument. Meekly, Timmy took a seat.

He had the same awful feeling he'd had when he'd been sent to the principal's office.

"All right, young man, tell us what happened." His mother had taken over the questioning now.

"I was playing a game at the arcade and it broke. I don't know how it happened. It was an accident."

"The arcade owner told me even a professional wrestler couldn't have broken the machine. He said you must have broken it on purpose. What do you have to say to that?"

Timmy could think of nothing to say. He wasn't about to tell his parents that their son was a freak, stronger than ten professional wrestlers rolled into one. Or that he was so strong he could pick both of them up and lift them over his head, if he chose to. Or that he was so powerful, he couldn't play a game right if he tried — softball, Bicep Buster, or anything else, probably.

So he said nothing.

"I don't know what's come over you, Timmy," his mother said, looking puzzled. "You have never caused us problems before. This incident at the arcade is bad enough. But I washed your clothes today, and discovered you ripped your pants again. This, after I told you to be more careful with your clothes."

Timmy's father took over.

"Money doesn't grow on trees, Timmy. You're going to have to learn to be more responsible. Maybe that lesson will sink in if you stay home and think about it some more. Which is exactly what you're going to do.

"I'm sorry, son, but you're grounded."

Chapter Twenty-One

For the next four weeks, Timmy was to go home directly from school. On weekends, he had to stay home, too, unless he got his mother's or father's permission to leave the house. And even then he could only go to places like the library.

Timmy's parents also cut back his television and telephone privileges. He could watch only one hour of television a day. He was limited to one telephone call a week, for no longer than twenty minutes.

Yes, Timmy thought to himself, he certainly did have plenty of time to think about being more responsible. The problem was, he didn't know what he could have done differently to avoid the jam he was in.

The truth was, Timmy couldn't harness his new strength. And no amount of thinking about it was going to change that.

The day after the Bicep Buster incident,

Timmy was back at school. As he feared, nearly everybody in class had heard about it.

One of the first kids to come up to him was Hank.

"Way to go man," he said with a big grin. "I really underestimated you. Maybe you ought to start hanging with me and my pals."

Oh great, Timmy thought. Now a thug thinks I'm cool. That's just what I don't need.

Before class began, Timmy asked Sally if she wanted to eat lunch with him later.

"Um, I don't think so, Timmy. I've already made plans."

That morning, it seemed to Timmy that his teacher was keeping a close eye on him. He might have imagined it, but it wouldn't be surprising if she were. He had a bad reputation now, and he didn't like it.

Once a quiet bookworm, Timmy was now coming to be known as a rough-and-tumble kid to steer clear of.

The morning was uneventful. Timmy knew the right answer every time his teacher called on him. At least his new-found strength hadn't affected his brain, he thought.

At lunch, Timmy walked to the cafeteria with Howard. Most of the kids were already seated and eating.

Including Sally, who was eating alone in a corner.

Timmy felt his face get hot. He was embarrassed and angry. He knew Sally had lied when she said she had plans for lunch. It was clear to him now that she just didn't want anything to do with the new Timmy.

His thoughts were interrupted by Howard.

"What's the matter with you? Your face is red. Are you sick?

"No, I'm all right," Timmy fibbed. "Let's eat."

At lunch, Hank came over and joined Timmy and Howard.

"Hey, Timmy, what say we go to the arcade after school? We'll have a blast!"

Timmy wanted nothing to do with Hank, but he didn't want to be rude, either. Luckily, he could get out of this by telling the truth.

"I can't, Hank. Mr. Morales told me to never come back there. I guess the arcade is off limits to me forever."

This impressed Hank. Even he had never been

banned from the arcade, or any place else.

"Okay, then let's just hang out at the mall. We can play with stuff at the sporting goods store until they make us leave."

"Sorry Hank, but I'm grounded. I can't go anywhere after school."

"All right. We'll do it some other time."

Once again, Timmy declined to join those of his classmates who were going to play softball during the rest of the lunch hour. By now, he was afraid to do anything that might involve using his strength.

Instead, he and Howard decided to watch the others play. Before they headed out to the school yard, Timmy stopped at a cafeteria vending machine. He wanted a lemonade.

When Timmy deposited his money and pushed the button, the lemonade carton started to drop, but then stopped.

This had happened before to Timmy and his classmates. They would jiggle the machine or hit it with a palm of the hand, and usually the drink would fall.

So when Timmy's drink didn't come down the chute, he did what he had always done before.

Maybe it was because he was still smarting

over Sally rejecting him. Or maybe he was still feeling frustrated over being grounded by his parents. Whatever the reason, Timmy hit the machine harder than usual. He forgot he was now super-strong.

Everybody in the cafeteria heard what happened next.

Ka-POW!

The noise was like an explosion, echoing through the cafeteria. Some kids hit the floor and hid under tables. A few thought the sound was a gunshot. Others feared a wall was caving in.

It was neither.

The sound was made by Timmy's hand going right through the drink machine.

<u>Chapter Twenty-Two</u>

Timmy looked first at his hand, then at the vending machine.

What he saw was such a shock it took him a moment to realize what had happened. The noise when he had shattered the vending machine had been sickening!

He shuddered.

A crowd of kids gathered around him, but they didn't come too close. The boy that Hank had called Timid Timmy was now Terrible Timmy. Nobody dared mock him now.

"Did you see that?" Timmy heard somebody murmur.

"Timmy's in big trouble now!" said another voice.

Then came a voice he recognized. It was Hank's.

"Cool, Timmy," he laughed.

A teacher who had been in the cafeteria, Mrs. Young, was not laughing. She marched over to Timmy and grabbed him by the arm.

"Come with me, young man!" she ordered.

Mrs. Young escorted Timmy to a place he was beginning to know well — the office of Mr. Halpern, the principal.

Mrs. Young explained to Mr. Halpern that Timmy had smashed the cafeteria vending machine. The machine, she added, was heavily damaged. Maybe even destroyed.

Mr. Halpern shook his head sadly.

"Destroying school property again, eh Timmy?"

The principal called to his secretary in the next office: "Doris, get me Timmy's home telephone number."

A minute later, the secretary entered Mr. Halpern's office and gave him the phone number. Mr. Halpern dialed it at once and asked Timmy's mother to come to the school right away.

"It's urgent," he told her in a grave voice.

Timmy waited outside Mr. Halpern's office for his mother to arrive. Half an hour later, she strode through the door. She looked very worried.

She saw Timmy sitting in the chair. But before she could ask him what he was doing there, Mr. Halpern invited her into his office. "You come in, too, Timmy," he said.

Mr. Halpern proceeded to tell Timmy's mother about how her son had demolished the vending machine in the cafeteria. Then he told her that Timmy also seemed to have tossed a softball over the school yard fence.

Timmy's mother looked pale. She seemed to have trouble believing everything she was hearing.

Timmy thought she might cry.

"I don't understand why this is happening, Mr. Halpern," she stammered.

"Nor do I," replied the principal in an oily voice.

As Timmy's mother sat, nervously wringing her hands, Mr. Halpern outlined what he thought should be done about Timmy.

"First, he may not return to class today. You must take him home. We cannot have Timmy disrupting the other students.

"Second, starting tomorrow, Timmy will have to stay after school every day to help our janitor, Mr.

King, with his chores. Just as he did recently. Only this time, Timmy must do this two hours a day for two weeks.

"Third, I'm afraid you and Timmy's father will have to pay to repair or replace the vending machine Timmy broke. You might want to consider deducting some of the total from Timmy's allowance."

Timmy's mother nodded her head numbly.

"There is one other thing, I should have mentioned," Mr. Halpern added.

"Yes?"

"If we have any more problems like this with Timmy, he will be expelled."

Timmy's mother began to cry.

Chapter Twenty-Three

Timmy spent the rest of the afternoon in his bedroom, waiting for his father to come home from work.

When he arrived, Timmy could hear muffled voices from the kitchen as his mother explained what had happened.

Then came the words Timmy had been dreading: "Son, get out here right now!"

Once again, Timmy's parents tried to understand why their son had suddenly become a problem student. Once again, Timmy was vague. He insisted he hadn't meant to lose the school's softball or break the vending machine. Just like he hadn't meant to destroy the Bicep Buster at the arcade.

Timmy's answers did not satisfy his father. Not even a little bit.

"If I had the money, I would send you to military school in Danville," his father shouted. "You would learn a thing or two there about discipline! About responsibility!"

Timmy shuddered at the thought. His heart beat faster with fear. One more mishap, and maybe somehow his father would *find* the money.

Danville was a hundred miles away. He would have to live in a dormitory. He would see his family and friends only on weekends.

Up early in the morning. Wearing a uniform. Polishing his shoes every single day. Answering, "Yes, Sir!" when instructors shouted in his face.

The strict regimen did not appeal to Timmy at all. He knew he would hate it. He shivered again, just at the thought.

"But I can't afford to send you there," his father fumed. "Especially now that I have to pay for the gol-darned arcade game and the vending machine you broke!"

Timmy's parents doubled the time he was grounded from four weeks to eight weeks. He could watch no television and receive no phone calls during this time. None. Zero.

When he went to bed that night, Timmy lay awake for a long time.

He thought about what fun it had been at first to be so strong.

He'd had no need to fear Hank. Instead of being the boy nobody wanted on their softball team, he was the player *everybody* wanted. And he had loved the way everybody had been in awe of him after he sent the Hi-Striker bell into orbit.

But now it had all turned bad.

Today was the last straw. He couldn't believe that he, one of the best students in his class, was on the verge of being expelled. How he wished he could go back to being the boy he used to be!

He felt like crying.

Lying in bed, staring at the ceiling, Timmy realized what he had to do. He had to find Myra the Mystic and ask her — beg her, if necessary — to lift the spell.

But now that he was grounded, he could not go anywhere after school.

After a while, Timmy heard his parents getting ready for bed. He was usually asleep before this. But tonight, he had something important on his mind. Something extremely important.

He was figuring out a way to visit Myra the Mystic again.

Chapter Twenty-Four

The next day at school, Timmy struggled to stay awake.

It had been past midnight when he had finally drifted off to sleep, and now he was paying for it.

All his classmates had heard about him breaking the juice machine. They combined this tale with accounts of his other feats of strength, such as hitting the softball out of the school yard and crushing the Bicep Buster.

With each telling, Timmy's exploits became even more fantastic. Some kids now claimed he had hit the softball so high that it hit a passing airplane. Others swore he not only broke the Bicep Buster, but several other games at the arcade, too.

Sally wouldn't even look at him any more. Even Howard seemed distant. When Timmy asked him if he wanted to eat lunch together, Howard said he was busy and walked away.

Only Hank was friendly toward Timmy — and for all the wrong reasons.

Timmy ate alone in a corner of the cafeteria. The juice machine still had a big hole in it, courtesy of his fist. Somebody had taped a handwritten note to the machine: "Out of order."

It occurred to Timmy that his whole life was out of order.

The rest of the day passed so slowly it seemed as if it would never end. Nobody spoke to Timmy. It was like being a new kid on his first day at school.

Then Timmy's day got worse.

After school, he visited the janitor, Mr. King, at his little office.

This time, Mr. King didn't have to explain to Timmy how to do the work. Timmy had become an old hand at it.

Once again, he cleaned toilets and emptied waste baskets. He swept floors, scrubbed stains and scraped gum. His back hurt from all the bending over. His hands had blisters from so much sweeping and mopping.

When he finished helping Mr. King, Timmy trudged home.

Tonight he planned to put into effect his plan to remove Myra's spell.

Thinking about the scheme made him nervous and excited at the same time.

At dinner, Timmy's parents said little. They were still angry and disappointed. And they were confused, unable to understand what had come over their son.

Timmy excused himself after dinner. He told his parents he was tired from his janitorial job and was going straight to bed.

He went to his room, closed the door and turned out the light. He really was tired, but he wasn't going to bed.

With the light off in his room, Timmy got his rolled-up sleeping bag out of his closet and placed it under the bed covers. He took his bulkiest clothes — sweaters, jackets and the like — and stuffed them under the covers too.

He arranged them this way and that. Then he pulled the covers up nearly to the pillow.

At last he was satisfied. If his parents looked in his room, there was a good chance they would be fooled into thinking Timmy was under the covers, sleeping.

Suddenly, he heard a soft knock on his bedroom door.

Timmy tiptoed quickly to his closet. Just as he closed the door behind him, the bedroom door opened.

He peeked out through a crack in the closet door. He could see his parents standing at the entrance to his room. His heart was beating so fast and so hard, he thought surely they could hear it.

They did not look toward the closet. But Timmy feared they would go over to the bed and take a closer look. If they did, he knew he would be in still bigger trouble — if that was possible.

"He must be asleep, already," he heard his mother murmur.

"I guess so," came the reply.

Timmy's parents lingered a moment longer.

Timmy held his breath.

Then they turned around and closed the door behind them.

Timmy heaved a sigh of relief.

He went to his window and slowly lifted it. It had not been opened for a couple of months, and it creaked loudly. Timmy scampered back to the closet, thinking his parents must have heard it.

When his parents did not return, he turned back to the window. Again, he lifted it, until it was open most of the way. Then he removed the screen.

He took a deep breath, and made his move. He crawled out the window and jumped to the ground with a soft thud.

He was heading back to the carnival.

Chapter Twenty-Five

Timmy needed to find Myra the Mystic. Tonight.

This was the carnival's last night in town. As soon as it closed, at eleven p.m., the carnies would break down the booths, the rides, and the other attractions and load them onto trailers and trucks which would take them to the next town on their circuit.

Timmy walked quickly in the direction of the carnival.

He glanced at his watch. It already was nearly nine o'clock.

The carnival was only a few blocks away, but he had little time to find Myra. He walked even faster.

When he arrived, he paid the admission and headed down the midway toward Myra's tiny cottage.

The carnival wasn't as crowded as it had been on Friday night. This being a week night, fewer people were here because they had to go to work or school the next day, Timmy figured. And a lot of people had already been to the carnival during the past few days.

He walked past a series of joints featuring games of skill and chance. He saw a half-dozen people lined up at the glass pitch booth.

Each player was given ten dimes for a dollar. They tossed the dimes at plates, goblets, glasses, ashtrays and small bowls. Whenever a dime landed in something, that was what the player won.

Most of the time, the dimes missed or bounced out of whatever they landed in. Still, some of the players had won three or four prizes, Timmy noticed.

At the next joint was a similar game called the Spot Pitch. Here, the players lobbed dimes onto a large, flat board covered with red Lucky Strike decals.

To win a small prize, a player had to get the dime completely inside the red circle of the decal. Timmy had played this game last year with little luck. It seemed like his dimes always overlapped with the part of the board outside the red circles.

But there was no time for games tonight.

He had to find Myra the Mystic. Fast.

He continued down the midway toward the darkened area where he had found Myra.

He hoped she wouldn't be mad that he wanted the spell lifted. But even if she was, Timmy planned to insist she do so. The spell had to be lifted, or his life would be ruined.

He continued past a shooting gallery and a game where you had to pop balloons with darts to win a prize.

Timmy saw the Water Race game, where he had tricked Hank and his friends into chasing him into a trap near the Haunted House.

He avoided the place now. He was afraid the Water Race operator would have him kicked out of the carnival if he saw him.

He passed a few rides like the Octopus and the Hammer. Now he recognized where he was.

Just a few more yards and he would come to Myra's strange little house. At last, he could get the spell removed and go back to being the boy he used to be.

Timmy walked faster with growing excitement. Myra the Mystic's cabin was just ahead.

Then, suddenly, he stopped. His mouth dropped open in shock.

The cabin was gone!

<u>Chapter Twenty-Six</u>

Timmy thought he must have made a mistake.

Surely, he was in the wrong place? He would get his bearings, figure out which direction he had to go, and find Myra's cabin.

He looked around.

The lights of the carnival flashed in the dark. The Ferris wheel circled overhead. Music from different rides mingled into an unintelligible blend. The carnies barked at customers, trying to lure them to their joints.

And Timmy's heart fell.

He was certain this was the right spot.

An empty space gaped where Myra's dimly lit home had stood. The space was hardly even noticeable, because Myra's place had taken up so little room.

Timmy's mind reeled.

He had to find Myra or he was doomed to a life of trouble. He would have accident after accident, followed by punishment after punishment. And when he got sent to military school, he'd have more accidents, and probably get sent to the brig, if they had one.

At the rate he was going, he would probably wind up spending the rest of his life in prison.

He took a deep breath and tried to calm himself.

It didn't help.

Frantic, he walked further up the midway.

Maybe she had moved to a better spot. One where more people would see her business.

He could not find her.

He turned around and headed back to where her cottage had been. Where she had been the night she had turned him into a freak.

He almost believed that when he returned, her cottage would somehow be there, as if by magic. Maybe he had somehow missed it.

He imagined the joy he would feel when he saw it.

But when he returned, he saw only the dark, empty area where Myra had set up shop earlier. He looked at his watch.

It was ten o'clock.

His stomach felt as if it were tied in knots. He felt short of breath. He was sweating even though the night was cool.

"What are you looking for kid?"

Timmy jumped.

He had been so lost in his thoughts he hadn't heard anybody come up behind him. The raspy voice in his ear had startled him badly.

He turned to find a frightening but familiar face staring at him.

It was the carny whose car he had lifted so the tire could be changed.

"I ... I'm l-l-looking for Myra the Mystic," Timmy stammered.

"She left town," the carny said. The raspy voice grated in Timmy's ears. He could not believe what he was hearing.

"She went on to our next stop," the carny said. "Said business was bad here, so she might as well leave. What do you want to see her for?"

Quickly, Timmy explained about the spell, and all the problems it had caused him.

"So that's how you could lift my car," the

carny rasped, shaking his head in amazement. "I knew Myra had certain powers, but I didn't know she was *that* good."

Timmy was devastated. Myra was gone. He was doomed to a life of detention and toilet-cleaning. Or maybe military school and its brig, which he imagined now was probably in a basement, like a dungeon. Or even a lifetime in prison — him, the star student, the bookworm, sharing a cell for fifty years with murderers and thieves and huge, hairy rats.

"Of course, there is one thing that might solve your problem," the carny continued.

"What is it?" Timmy asked. He was desperate, willing to try anything.

"Her daughter, Queenie. She's got some of her mother's powers. Least, that's what I hear."

"Where do I find her?" Timmy asked, his hopes soaring.

"She works inside the Haunted House. She's the ghoul with an ax in her head."

The carny began to tell Timmy more about Queenie, but Timmy had already begun running down the midway.

He ran as fast as he could. He did not notice the names of the rides or the games. He was barely aware of the colorful lights and the barrage of noise. When the carnies working at joints beckoned and yelled for him to play their games, he didn't even hear them.

His thoughts focused on one thing only — finding Myra's daughter and getting the spell removed.

Finally, he reached the Haunted House.

He was gasping so hard he could barely talk. He took three big gulps of air and asked the guy selling tickets if he could speak to Queenie.

The ticket seller leered at him and grinned.

"We ain't got nobody here named Queenie," he said.

<u>Chapter Twenty-Seven</u>

Timmy's heart sank.

If he could not find Queenie, all was lost. He was doomed.

He had to keep trying.

"But I was told you had a woman named Queenie working inside the Haunted House," he persisted. "She's supposed to have an ax in her head."

"Yeah, we got somebody in there like that," the man replied. "I don't know her name. For all I know, she's Demi Moore."

"Can I go in and see her?"

"Sure, kid, as long as you pay your dollar like everybody else. And don't wait too long. We're closing soon."

Timmy looked at his watch. It was a quarter to eleven! He fished through his pockets, found a crumpled dollar bill and gave it to the ticket seller.

Then he went inside the Haunted House.

He had to walk down dark, twisting, curving hallways and into many different rooms.

He could hardly see. He was the only customer. Mist filled the air.

A woman's blood-curdling screams pierced the darkness. Nearer, Timmy heard a man groaning. He sounded like he was being tortured.

Timmy knew these sounds were probably recordings.

Yet, he couldn't help feeling scared.

"Aaarrgh!"

Suddenly, an 8-foot tall monster with one eye and blood dripping from his face leaped out of a dark corner, right at Timmy.

Timmy jumped back. For a moment, his heart stopped beating. The hair on his neck stood on end.

"Aaarrgh!" the monster bellowed again.

Timmy hurried on. He was relieved that the monster did not follow him.

The house was so dark he had to feel his way along the hallway. The fog swirled.

A woman's voice cried, "Help me! Help me!"

Timmy peered into the gloom. He could see nothing.

Suddenly, a room ahead of him lit up. A body was hanging from a noose. Just as suddenly, the room went dark again.

A voice near the gallows laughed maniacally.

Timmy didn't like this place one bit. But he had no time to think about it. Stepping up to him out of the gloom was a horribly disfigured woman.

She had warts and scars on her face. Her eyes had black circles around them. Her hair had never seen a comb.

And she had an ax lodged in the side of her head. Blood dripped down her ear.

Timmy heard himself scream. But he recovered quickly.

"Are you Queenie?" he asked.

The ugly face looked surpised.

"Who are you?" it asked.

Timmy explained about Myra's spell. He told about the trouble he had been getting in, and how desperate he was to have the spell removed. He had not been able to find Myra, but he had been told that she — Myra's daughter — might be able help him.

The ghoul shook her head dubiously.

"I don't know if I can," she said.

"Please!" Timmy pleaded. "It's important!"

"We close in a few minutes," Queenie said. "Meet me behind this place in ten minutes."

Timmy left as quickly as he could.

He waited in the dark beind the Haunted House. Minutes passed. He tapped his toe nervously in the dirt.

Finally, Queenie came out the back door, the garish makeup still caked on her face. The ax was still stuck in her head.

"My trailer is right over there," she said, pointing to the parking lot. "Let's go there."

Timmy followed her into the tiny trailer. In the light, he could see that the blood oozing from the ax was not real, and neither was the ax.

In fact, he could tell that, without the scary makeup, Queenie wouldn't be bad looking at all.

"Here's the problem," Queenie said, studying Timmy. "My mother — Myra — has been teaching me the secrets of being a mystic, but I'm still a novice. I know how to do a few things, but not all the stuff she can do.

"I can try to remove the spell, but I don't know if it will work. Or it might work, but I could accidentally cast another spell on you. You could end up losing your super strength, but you might take on the traits of a coyote or a cow. It's happened before. You see, removing a spell and creating a spell that turns somebody into an animal, involve very similar techniques. I'm still learning how to do this."

Timmy took a deep breath and answered.

"I'll take the chance," he said. "I have just got to be rid of this spell."

Queenie told Timmy to sit across from her at a small table. She did not rub any oils on him, as her mother had.

She told him to close his eyes. Then she chanted in a strange language, her voice growing louder and louder. She held one hand firmly on Timmy's head. It actually hurt.

"You can open your eyes, now," she said after a few minutes. "It is done."

"Did it work?" Timmy asked anxiously. His heart was hammering in his throat. He had to know the answer.

"It's too early to tell. You will know by morning. Now you must go. I have to get ready to move on to the next town."

Timmy stumbled outside. It was 11:30, well past his normal bed time. He ran down the midway, which already was being dismantled. Timmy continued to run, all the way home.

As he walked up to his house, he saw that it was dark inside. His parents had gone to bed. Timmy breathed a sigh of relief. If they had discovered he wasn't in bed, they would still be up, worrying about him and looking for him.

Timmy tiptoed around to his bedroom, climbed in the window and put the screen back in place.

He took the sleeping bag and clothing out of his bed and lay down. For a few minues, he worried that Queenie had failed to lift the spell.

Then he sank into a deep sleep.

Chapter Twenty-Eight

"Timmy! Wake up! Do you hear me? Wake up!"

Timmy opened his eyes to find his mother hunched over his bed, shaking him by the shoulder.

"You slept through your alarm. You're going to be late for school if you don't hurry. Get up right now."

Timmy sat up groggily. Then he remembered his visit last night to the carnival and Queenie.

Had she removed the spell? Did it work?

"Okay, mom," he said, suddenly more alert. "I'll be ready for breakfast in a few minutes."

As soon as his mother left, Timmy leaped out of bed and hurried to the corner of his room. There stood the cigar store Indian— the same heavy statue Timmy had lifted over his head after he had visited Myra the Mystic. The same statue that Timmy used to be unable to lift even an inch off the floor.

Timmy placed his arms around the base of the cigar store Indian and lifted with all his might.

The statue didn't budge.

Maybe I didn't get a good grip on it, Timmy thought.

He bent down, wrapped his arms around the Indian and lifted again.

Nothing. The statue didn't move.

Timmy was elated. Queenie had removed the spell! Timmy could be his old self again!

He looked in the mirror. Queenie had not turned him into a coyote or a cow. He sounded just like he always did. Yes, indeed! It had worked!

He joined his parents for breakfast. He felt as if a huge weight had been lifted from his shoulders. He had not smiled in several days, but now he could not stop grinning.

"I won't be getting into any more trouble from now on," he told his parents confidently.

His parents looked at each other. They seemed to think the punishment had finally made Timmy straighten up.

"We hope not, son," his father said.

Timmy was still smiling when he arrived at

school that morning. Once again, it was fun being at school — now that he no longer had to worry about his super strength getting him into trouble.

His classmates could sense the change.

Sally smiled shyly at him. From across the classroom, Howard gave him a little wave.

His teacher wasn't sure what to make of Timmy's smiling. She wondered if he had hatched some new scheme to destroy school property.

She decided to call on Timmy soon. Maybe that would help her figure out what he was up to. She began discussing the day's math lesson and wrote an equation on the blackboard.

Then she turned and faced the class.

"Timmy, do you know the answer?"

Timmy smiled again. Yes, he knew the answer. He loved being called on in class to solve a problem. Before he had super strength, it was the only way he could ever show off in front of his classmates.

He opened his mouth to respond.

Suddenly, he dropped to the floor on all fours and threw his head into the air. The mournful sound that came out of his mouth shocked him and terrified the entire class.

"Ow-ooooo! Ow-oooooo!"

BE SURE TO READ THESE OTHER
COLD, CLAMMY SHIVERS BOOKS.

A GHASTLY SHADE
OF GREEN

JASON'S MOTHER TAKES HIM AND HIS
LITTLE BROTHER ON A VACATION TO
FLORIDA – BUT NOT TO THE BEACH. SHE
RENTS A LONELY CABIN ON THE EDGE
OF THE EVERGLADES, WHERE THE
ALLIGATORS BELLOW AND THE PLANTS
GROW SO THICK THEY ALMOST BLOT
OUT THE LIGHT. JASON DOES NOT LIKE
THIS PLACE AT ALL. AND STRANGE
THINGS START TO HAPPEN: KEEPSAKES
DISAPPEAR FROM HIS DRESSER. HIS
BEAGLE WINDS UP MISSING. AT FIRST
JASON SUSPECTS BURGLARS, BUT THE
TRUTH IS MORE FRIGHTENING. JASON
MUST MAKE A DESPERATE EFFORT TO
SAVE HIS FAMILY – AND HIMSELF.

BE SURE TO READ THESE OTHER COLD, CLAMMY SHIVERS BOOKS.

THE HAUNTING HOUSE

WHEN CAITLIN MOVES INTO AN OLD HOUSE, SHE HAS A STRANGE FEELING SHE IS DISTURBING THE HOUSE'S PEACE. SHE IS BOTHERED BY STRANGE NOISES. WEIRD THINGS START TO HAPPEN. THINGS THAT CANNOT BE EXPLAINED. AT FIRST CAITLIN THINKS THE HOUSE MAY BE HAUNTED. BUT SHE SOON STARTS TO WONDER IF THERE IS SOMETHING AT WORK EVEN MORE FRIGHTENING THAN GHOSTS – AND MORE DANGEROUS. ALL SHE KNOWS FOR SURE IS THIS: SOME FRIGHTENING PRESENCE IN HER NEW HOME IS ALSO DEADLY.